Bradley United Methodist Church
PENNSYLVANIA AND MAIN STREETS
GREENFIELD, INDIANA 46140

ERIC and MATILDA

by Mischa Richter

HARPER & ROW, PUBLISHERS, NEW YORK, EVANSTON, AND LONDON

To my sons Daniel and Thomas

ERIC AND MATILDA

Copyright © 1967 by Mischa Richter

Printed in the United States of America. All rights reserved. No part of this book may be used or reproduced in any manner whatsoever without written permission except in the case of brief quotations embodied in critical articles and reviews. For information address Harper & Row, Publishers, Incorporated, 49 East 33rd Street, New York, N. Y. 10016.

Library of Congress Catalog Card Number: 67-21572

Eric was watching a parade.
He noticed Matilda, a very charming young goose
who was marching in it.

He decided to join the parade and march near her.

She didn't seem to notice Eric.

I must show her I love her, he thought.

He wanted her to look at him.

He tried marching backward.

But Matilda didn't pay any attention to him.

He marched on his head.

But Matilda didn't seem to care.

He fell behind her and tried singing.

But Matilda didn't seem to hear him.

He ran ahead and tried marching
with his wings above his head.

But Matilda marched on.

Finally he got discouraged and took a walk in the woods.

He wanted to think things over.

He told his troubles to an owl.
"Why not try telling her you love her?"
said the owl wisely.

18

So Eric went back to rejoin the parade.
But when he got there...

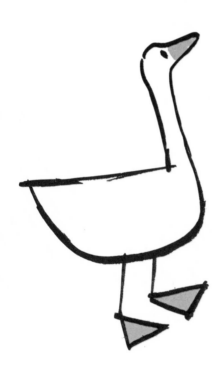

he saw geese taking off in great flights over his head.

Matilda too.

He soared up.

"Matilda," he called.

"Matilda, wait. I love you."

Matilda turned her graceful neck.
"Eric," she said.

"I didn't know you knew my name," said Eric.
"I thought you'd never noticed me.

I walked backward, I marched on my head,
I sang, I held my wings up.
You never noticed."

"I noticed you the first day you came.
I saw you do those things," Matilda said shyly.

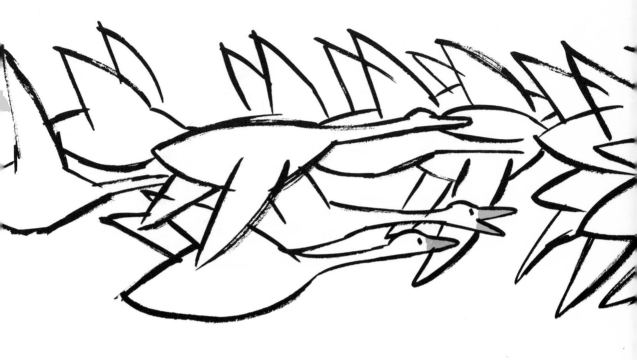

"But I didn't know you loved me
till you told me just now.

I love you too."

And they flew south together,

wing to wing.

J

Richter, Mischa

Eri~~c~~ ~~Ma~~tilda

AUTHOR	
Richter, Mischa	
TITLE	
Eric & Matilda	
DATE DUE	BORROWER'S NAME
Feb 23	D Frank
1/76	Frank
NOV 1 4 1976	E Potter
EC 12 1976	preschool
JAN 16 1977	
NOV 2 7 1977	pr-